David Elliott

THE TIGER'S BACK

David Elliott is a *New York Times* bestselling author of books for young people including *In the Wild, On the Farm,* and *Finn Throws a Fit!*. His middle grade novels include *The Transmogrification of Roscoe Wizzle,* The Evangeline Mudd books, and most recently, *Jeremy Cabbage and the Living Museum of Human Oddballs and Quadruped Delights.* David teaches writing at Colby-Sawyer College and Lesley University's MFA Program in Creative Writing. He is currently working on a collection of short stories.

First published by GemmaMedia in 2011.

GemmaMedia
230 Commercial Street
Boston, MA 02109 USA

www.gemmamedia.com

Printed in the United States of America

15   14   13   12   11   1   2   3   4   5

978-1-936846-05-4

Library of Congress Cataloging-in-Publication Data

Cover by Night & Day Design

Inspired by the Irish series of books designed for adult literacy, Gemma Open Door Foundation provides fresh stories, new ideas, and essential resources for young people and adults as they embrace the power of reading and the written word.

Brian Bouldrey
North American Series Editor

GEMMA
Open Door

For a man, a monkey, and a banana

ONE

One Mississippi. Two Mississippi.

When Robert closed his eyes, he could see them. Each rolling along after the next. Like the cars on a toy train. Seven words. So simple a child could understand.

But the words weren't the problem. It was the sentence they formed. He couldn't make sense of it.

Keep it together, old boy, he told himself. *You're having a senior moment. That's all.*

He was standing in his own kitchen. Fingers gripping the broad lip of the farmer's sink Claire had chosen when they bought the house. The porcelain, cool and familiar under his hand, was still unblemished after all these years.

How many times had he admired it? And how many hours had Claire stood there, just where he stood now? Humming, her eyes lifted to the window as she rinsed a cup or dried a plate. Thousands, he'd bet, if you added them up. Maybe even more.

He spoke the sentence aloud.

There... is ... a... tiger... in... the... roses.

There is a tiger in the roses.

He opened his eyes. The water was still running. The glass was still in his hand. And the tiger was still standing in the roses. Exactly as it had been when he had risen from his morning nap, awakening with a terrible thirst.

Terrific! he said aloud. *I'm seeing things. What next?*

The tiger, all ember and ash, must have weighed five hundred pounds. It shifted this weight to its haunches and sat down almost as if it had asked the same question. What next?

It had to be some trick of the light. The way the sun was shining through the hemlocks. Or maybe he was still half asleep. Maybe that was it. Maybe he was still dreaming.

He set the glass in the sink, looked down at the pine floorboards and counted. Taking his time. Forcing himself as he had when a boy playing Ghost-in-the-Graveyard with the Kennedy kids next door.

One Mississippi.

Two Mississippi.

He looked up.

It was impossible! The tiger was under the arbor now! Smashing his prized William Baffins. Or were the roses Henry Hudsons? He wasn't sure. They were named after a northern explorer, though. He was certain of *that*. He might be losing his mind, but he knew *that* much.

He blinked. The creature blinked back and it occurred to him that the tiger was having as much trouble understanding him as he was the tiger. But that was ridiculous! This was *his* house. *His* garden. Those were *his* roses, whatever their name. He had planted them. Watered them when they needed it. Weeded them when the burdock took over.

Or had every year until this one. This summer Miles had done all that. But still. That wasn't the point.

The point was that *he* belonged here. The tiger did not! This was Vermont! The Green Mountain State. Birthplace of not one but *two* presidents. So what if one of them was Chester Alan Arthur? That only proved it! It was the opposite of places where tigers roamed around snatching rice farmers out of their huts. India or Sumatra or Bangladesh. (He was sure there *were* tigers in Bangladesh. He remembered seeing a special about it on public television.)

Anyway, hadn't the Chinese eaten all the tigers? Or used them in their medicine? Hadn't he read that somewhere?

Medicine.

Yes! That had to be it.

His medicine.

Or as everyone else called it, his *medication*.

He lowered his eyes to the windowsill. Some of the bottles were white, the color of spoiled milk. Others were a harsh, translucent green. Lined up against the maple sash, they formed a miniature skyline. A science fiction notion of a future metropolis. How ironic, then, that the bottle-city on his windowsill *did* represent a future. His. Or what was left of it anyway.

And, unfortunately for Robert, it was not a city whose residents always got along. What had the doctors warned him about? Counter-indications? Wasn't that it? But had any of them actually mentioned hallucinations? That's what he wanted to know now. Had any of them said anything about seeing jungle cats in your William Baffins?

He tried to remember, but the doctors talked so much. And for all he understood, they might as well have been speaking Martian. Anyway, it didn't matter. The details weren't important. He'd decided that early on. When he first heard the diagnosis. Something bad was happening. That was all he needed to know. Something very, very bad.

He turned his gaze back to the arbor. The tiger yawned.

Maybe if he stepped away from the window. Maybe if he did something else, thought about something else. Maybe if he did that, when he came back to the window, the tiger would be gone. And he could forget about it.

Okay.

Not *forget* about it.

But *accept* it at least.

The last couple of years had taught him that. The last couple of years had taught him that he could accept anything. No matter how absurd, how impossible.

Claire's fading away like that.

The devastating news of his own illness.

Was a tiger on the lawn any more shocking?

TWO

No Dice

He stepped away from the window and over to the refrigerator. It was relatively new. But it was white, not stainless steel—*It's a kitchen, not a hospital,* Claire had said—and had none of the gadgets that the salesman tried to convince them they needed. Ice dispensers and so on.

A sheet of paper hung on the door. The paper was pink, the color of sherbet and held in place by a Santa Claus magnet. One of the oncologists had given him this. The paper, not the magnet.

"Your Side Effects Diary," the doctor had said, smiling as if she were handing

9

him a premiums package from one of those time-share companies.

She went on to explain that using the symbols listed down the left margin, he was to keep a day-to-day record of how he was feeling. Then sum up the whole before he went to bed by circling either a Smiley Face (Feel Good), a Frowny Face (Feel Bad) or a third face whose mouth was a simple straight line, no bigger than a dash.

The doctor had said this indicated Feel the Same. But to Robert it looked like Feel Perplexed. When he told her this, her smile wilted. She was very young. For a fraction of a second she looked exactly like the childish drawing they were talking about.

Later, it occurred to him that one of

those—what were they called?—Miles had told him… emo… emo… emoticons? Yes! That was it. Emoticons. It occurred to him that one of those emoticons might serve as the perfect epitaph. No words on the gravestone. Just the face. But which one? Feel Good? Feel Bad? Feel Perplexed? That's what he hadn't been able to decide. Which one?

He read through the list.

D – Diarrhea
DS – Dry Skin
F – Fatigue
Fe – Fever
H – Headache
HL – Hair Loss·
I – Infection

LA – Loss of Appetite
LC – Lack of Concentration
N – Nausea
V – Vomiting

He'd been hoping to find Ha—
Hallucinations. But ND. No Dice. Not
a word about seeing one of the four great
cats in your roses. But that had to be
it, didn't it? The medicine, he meant.
Or maybe it was the sign of something
worse. Maybe the cancer had set up
camp in his brain. It had invaded every
other part of his body. Why not there,
too? Why not central command?

He should do something. Tell some-
one. Call a doctor. But there were so
many of them he had lost track of who
was who. And how would he put it?

Hello. May I speak to Doctor Krishna or Doctor Singh or Doctor Goswami? (Was it some new law that all doctors had to be Indian?) *This is Robert Stevenson. Yes, Robert Louis Stevenson.* (His father thought *Treasure Island* the greatest book ever written.) *Woke up this morning.* (Feel Good.) *Had a little diarrhea.* (Feel Bad.) *Saw a tiger in my flower garden.* (Feel Perplexed.)

No. He wouldn't mention it. Not yet. He'd give it a day or two. See what happened.

He opened the refrigerator. More bottles. The ones that needed to be kept cool. A jar of picles. A roast chicken.

If only Claire were here. She would know exactly what to say. What to do. She would help him make sense of it.

Just as she always had. But there would be plenty of time for that later. Plenty of time to think of Claire. He was saving them up. His memories. They would see him through when the time came.

He shut the refrigerator and went back to the window, careful not to turn his gaze to the garden. Not yet. He closed his eyes once more. He breathed deeply. Once. Twice. Three times.

He opened his eyes.

THREE

Just Like Wild Kingdom

The tiger was gone, of course.

Robert leaned forward, his nose practically touching the mullions. He scanned the garden, the entire lawn. Nothing. The freshly mown grass as domestic as a handkerchief. As tame as a chessboard. The William Baffins—he was sure of it now, they *were* William Baffins—looked exactly as they always did this time of year. Not at all as if they had been trampled by something striped and wild.

But just because he couldn't see it now didn't mean that the tiger hadn't been there. It could have moved. Could

15

have loped off into the woods. Or into the barn. He looked toward the kitchen door and the screened breezeway that connected the barn to the house.

He knew that sometimes a black bear might break into a dwelling. If it was hungry enough. In fact, that very thing happened five or six years ago over in Barnard. Just a couple of towns away.

He and Claire had read all about it in *The Circulator*. Front page. The homeowner left a forty-pound bag of birdseed next to a window in a mudroom. A Flatlander. Naturally. From Boston. The bear crashed right through the screen. Gorged itself on the birdseed. Then decided to see what the kitchen might offer. They'd had to call the Fish and Game.

Dart guns and everything. *Just like on Wild Kingdom*, Claire had said.

It was a shame, though, because in the end, they killed the bear. Shot it. Said it was a danger to the community. A rogue.

Miles said they should have shot the Flatlander. Robert agreed with the boy. Especially because they'd done it while the bear was still unconscious from whatever drug the dart delivered. To Robert, this seemed a much worse crime than the bear's. He'd thought about writing a letter to the editor. *When?* he'd wanted to ask. *Just when had it become rogue to follow your nature?*

He thought about locking the door. Better safe than sorry, right? But where were the keys? He didn't know. In fact, he couldn't remember the last time he and Claire had locked the house. They'd even left it open when they went on that tour to Japan.

But it was crazy to be thinking of such things. Foolishness. There *was* no tiger. He'd just had a slight moment of... of what? He didn't like to call it insanity. He hadn't lost his marbles. Not in the slightest. He still knew who he was. Where he was. It was just an episode. What his good old grandmother used to call "a spell." He'd had a little spell. That was all. Nothing to worry about.

Robert picked up the glass he'd put down earlier and stuck it under the tap. The faucet still open, the water still running.

It was his one extravagance, this water. He loved the look of it gushing from the tap. Its sound, like a librarian's long *shush*. Loved knowing that it bubbled up from a cold, dark reservoir two hundred feet beneath the surface of the lawn. And loved knowing, too, that never, not once, had that reservoir threatened to run dry. Even during the drought. All his neighbors had come to him. Empty milk jugs in hand. He'd filled every one, and still had enough to water his garden. The rest of the state was a moonscape that year. But his lawn had stayed as green as County Kildare.

Or Bangladesh.

The water ran into the glass until it splashed over the sides, wetting his fingers. He lifted the glass to his lips and drank it down.

Maybe the whole thing with the tiger was because he'd been so thirsty. Didn't people dying of thirst in the desert see things? Things that weren't there? Isn't that what mirages were all about?

The trouble was he hadn't been dying of thirst when he got up from that nap.

Just dying.

He set the glass in the sink and shut off the tap.

FOUR

Home to the Clouds

Yes, he was dying. He knew that. Had known it for a while. The doctors hadn't told him so. Not directly. But there was something in the way they greeted him. The way they touched him. As if they were afraid their fingers might break through his thinning flesh. As if they knew that just beneath the surface he was rotting. From the inside out. Like a peach.

He took one of the bottles from the shelf, opened it, and expertly tapped out two capsules. They were the size of peas, but blue, like the Caribbean. *Why?* he wondered. *Why turquoise?* Were the tropical blues, the hot pinks and the lurid reds of the various pills he took throughout the

21

day meant to cheer him? Meant to make the whole thing easier to swallow?

He popped them in his mouth.

But he wasn't ungrateful. He didn't doubt that the doctors' concern was genuine. And he appreciated it. Even if sometimes he could barely understand what they were saying. Those Indian accents! But he also came to recognize what they were trying so hard to hide from him. And from themselves. *Thank god,* they were thinking. *It's not me. It's not me this time.*

He scanned the yard again.

One of the things he and Claire loved about this house was its situation smack at the top of a slow-rising five acres. The hill was nothing compared to its cousins further north. But it climbed high enough to make the sky visible from every window in the house. You didn't even have to look up. *It's like living on an island*, Claire had said the first time the realtor took them through.

Today, billowing clouds crammed the upper panes. Like piles of laundry waiting to be folded. Or an illustration from a child's picture book.

Yes, he thought, *exactly like a children's book*. Fanciful creatures lived in those clouds. Gryphons and unicorns. Dragons and mermaids. Real animals, too, of course. Elephants.

And tigers.

Perhaps that's where his tiger had come from. The sky. And perhaps that's where it had gone. Home. Home to the clouds.

FIVE

What He Wanted to Say

Robert didn't know how long he had been standing there when the phone rang. Three or four minutes. Maybe longer. The phone, impatient and shrill, sat on a small, round table in the corridor between the kitchen and the dining room. A piecrust table, it was called because of the raised scalloped edge.

Claire had looked all over for that table. Finally found it in antique shop down in Newfane. As Robert moved toward it, he tried to remember when phones stopped ringing and started chirping. He didn't approve.

He picked up the receiver. Probably a

telemarketer. Or maybe it was Miles. If so, he might tell him about the tiger.

But it was neither a seller nor Miles.

"Bob?"

His heart sank.

Why hadn't he signed up for that caller identification thing the phone company had tried to sell him?

"Bob? It's Mary Alice. Bob?"

Mary Alice Watkins lived on the green down in the village. Her husband, Ezra, was long dead. Went to bed one night and never got up. Robert had always suspected that the man had simply willed his heart to stop. Like one of those Buddhist monks. Certainly, the man had been a saint. He'd had to be to put up with Mary Alice for all those years.

"Bob? Are you there? Bob?"

He thought about not answering. Not hanging up, mind you. Just not answering. Stand there listening while she Bobbed herself to death.

"Bob?"

"Hello, Mary Alice."

"Oh, you *are* there! You had me worried, Bob. Thought I might have to come up there and make sure you were still with us. Is everything OK, Bob?"

Peachy, Mary Alice, he wanted to say. *Hunky-dory*.

He wanted to say his intestines felt as if they'd been scoured by a carpenter's rasp.

He wanted to say his doctors were poisoning him.

He wanted to say that not five minutes ago he had seen a man-eating tiger in his flower garden. (Of course, he didn't know for sure if it was a man-eater. His understanding from that TV show was that some were, some weren't. But the effect would have been good.)

But most of all, he wanted to say, (*shout*, in fact), "For Chrissake, Mary Alice! I'm dying! My name is Robert! Stop calling me Bob."

When she repeated her question—*Is everything okay, Bob?*—what he actually said was, "All right."

"All right?" Mary Alice repeated. "Oh, Bob. Only all right?"

"I'm rather tired. That's all, Mary Alice. What can I do for you?"

"I'm just about to put up a nice big pot of lentils." Mary Alice never cooked. She always *put up*. "And I thought I'd—"

"I've got plenty to eat here, Mary Alice. More than I can handle, truth be told, and—"

"Nonsense, Bob! You've got to keep up your strength. Everyone knows that. When you're as sick as you are, you've got to keep up your strength. I'll bring it up this afternoon. With some biscuits. Homemade. About five."

"Mary Ali—"

"Bye-bye, Bob."

The line went dead.

He didn't hang up, but stood there, the receiver resting on his shoulder. It was impossible not to admire how good Mary Alice was at what she did. Got on one track and stayed on it. No matter what. And if she ran over you? That was *your* fault. She was as strong as a horse, too. Would probably live to be a hundred.

It was so utterly unfair. Claire slowly vanishing while Mary Alice and her ilk went on through eternity delivering their poisonous stews to the moribund. Like something out of Greek mythology.

But he knew better than to travel down that road. Life wasn't about fairness. Any six-year-old could tell you that. It was about longevity.

He replaced the receiver.

He'd worry later about Mary Alice. For now, he'd check for the tiger one last time. But even as he headed back to the kitchen, the awful woman's voice buzzed in his head.

Bob?

Bob?

Bob?

Which is the more terrifying? he wondered. *The tiger? Or people like Mary Alice Watkins?*

He honestly couldn't say.

SIX

Poison Arrows

The tiger was gone for good. Or so it seemed.

This should have made him happy. Should have brought some relief. It meant the hallucination—if that's what it was—had passed. Why then did he feel so let down?

Maybe his disappointment wasn't that the tiger had vanished, but that Mary Alice had appeared. *People are good, mostly*, he told himself. And he believed it. His life with Claire had taught him that. So why let Mary Alice get under his skin?

He didn't know.

Except that she seemed so sure of everything. So certain. It drove him crazy. Could life really be as simple as she made it out to be? What if she were right and all the people she made miserable wrong?

He looked at the clock. Eleven-fifteen. Miles would come by at one, and they would run some errands. What to do until then? He was tired. And his gut was acting up. But that business with the tiger had riled him. Who could sleep after such goings on? Watch TV, then? But at this hour it was only PFD. Programming for Dumbbells. Claire had come up with that.

He walked back into the living room with no clear idea why or what to do once he got there. He needed to sit down, though. Calm himself.

He moved to a wall of books that lined the north end of the room. Those bookshelves were the first improvement (after the sink) he and Claire had made to the house. It was Miles's dad, Art, who built them. Floor to ceiling. Miles had been just a boy then. No more than a toddler.

"Don't know why you folks need all the books," the man had grumbled. "We got a good library right down the village." But he'd done an excellent job. The sides and shelves at a perfect ninety degrees in spite of the various ways that the floor and ceiling in the old house angled off. And even now, the shelves carried their heavy load without the slightest buckle.

Robert moved to the far left end of the shelves.

They'd been finished for over a week before Art would even let them think about taking the books from their cartons. "That varnish has got to harden," he'd said, instructing them as if they were his apprentices. "You put them books up there too soon, you ruin the finish." Only after the dour man had given his permission were they allowed to shelve their collection.

They'd spent an entire day at it. Organizing. Alphabetizing. Separating the fiction from the nature writing. The poetry from the biographies. They'd stopped only to have lunch, a picnic on the floor in front of the shelves. The books piled in miniature towers around them. Like shrines. *We're Hindus*, Claire said. *Offering food at the feet of the gods.* (The food in this case: bread, cheese, dilly beans.)

Where he was standing now should have been the beginning of the fiction section. The lineup of authors reading something like:

Adams, Richard

Alcott, Louisa

Amis, Martin.

But the first author on the shelf was not Adams, Richard. It was Child, Julia. And next to her: Hemingway, Ernest. And next to Hemingway: Burroughs,

William. He read the titles: *Mastering the Art of French Cooking. A Moveable Feast. Naked Lunch.*

Claire.

Over the years, she had taken to reshelving the books. Grouping them into clusters according to some secret inner logic. He never knew when this idle practice would strike her. He'd come in the room to find her standing in front of Art's handiwork, a book or two in hand. Before he knew it, *Pride and Prejudice* was snugged up next to *A History of Nazi Germany*.

He rested his fingertips against the books.

Last week, a visiting nurse had come to the house. A skinny woman, with a pierced nose and some kind of tattoo running around her ankle. Apparently, also a believer in that Chinese nonsense about where to put your sofa.

She'd walked into the room like a pirate boarding a prized schooner. But when she saw the books, she stopped dead in her tracks and backed up toward the kitchen. "You ought to put those books in a closed space," she'd scolded. "Behind doors. Too much sharp energy. They're shooting poison arrows at you."

A nurse! Of all people! Talking such foolishness! What was the world coming to? When he pointed out that it seemed to him *she* was the one with the poison arrows, she hadn't understood. Hadn't understood a thing.

But how could she have? How could she know that Claire had touched those books? That part of her was on each of their jackets. That she was sealed forever into each of their pages.

Even Miles had suggested he replace the books with some electronic doodad. A Candle. Or a Grendel. Or something ridiculous like that. "It'll hold up to thirty-five hundred books," he'd said. "Right at your fingertips."

Thirty-five hundred books? He didn't want thirty-five hundred books. Or need them. He wanted Claire. And he had her. Some of her anyway. Right there. Right there on the shelves.

SEVEN

Who Is Buried in Grant's Tomb?

He moved further down the wall of books. If they were shooting poison arrows at him, so be it. Get in line. Join the crowd.

He was hoping an old favorite would pop out at him. Or something he'd been meaning to read but forgotten about. It didn't make much difference what it was, really. Just something to help him forget about that tiger. And Mary Alice.

He didn't have the energy for anything too demanding. Not today. Hadn't been able to read Dickens or Eliot or any of them since he'd gotten sick.

Comfort. That's what he was after.

Some poetry then. Maybe something by that Polish poet with the unpronounce-able name. But where would Claire have stashed her?

He didn't have the energy to think about it. Or the heart. He reached the end of the bookcase empty-handed, un-til his eyes fell on a row of books with identical green bindings. Fake leather. Cheap gold lettering on the spines.

They'd bought the encyclopedias at a yard sale. Five bucks for the lot. It wasn't one of the big-name ones. Britannica or World Book. But it had done its job. Especially when it came to helping with the crosswords that both of them loved.

32 across: Burkina Faso before it was Burkina Faso. Answer: Upper Volta!

27 down: Hungarian Rasta dog. Answer: Komondor!

He took the first volume from its place.

A-B.

That was it! Just the thing he needed. William Baffin. Why not? He'd known who he was at one point. Looked him up when he bought the roses. But somewhere between Claire's Alzheimer's and his own cancer he'd forgotten. Might as well refresh his memory.

Book in hand, he walked across the room to his favorite chair. A swivel rocker the previous owners had left behind. Claire had it reupholstered in a manly stripe. Surprised him with it.

He sat down. Careful to keep his eyes away from the window behind him. No sense in getting anything started. Just when he was calming down.

Yes. William Baffin. Just the thing.

He opened the book.

Baffin, William. (1584–1622) English. Explored the Arctic Circle. Gave his name to Baffin Island.

Of course! He knew it! How could he have forgotten something as basic as that? It was like forgetting the answer to that old joke: Who is buried in Grant's tomb? It had to be the drugs.

He read on.

The earliest mention of Baffin is in connection with Denmark's King Christian IV's Expeditions to Greenland (1612) under the command of Captain James Hall, later killed in Greenland by local inhabitants. During the following two years Baffin served as a pilot in the Spitzbergen whale fishery.

What a life men lived then! Exploring. Whaling. Swashbuckling with Greenlanders. How different from his own.

And yet his own had not been without adventure. Adventure of a different sort, maybe. But no less exciting. Yes, the more he thought about it, the more he began to see himself as a kind of explorer. After all, he'd devoted much of life to trying to understand himself and those around him. Wasn't that a kind of adventure? And not just those he loved. Not just Claire. And Miles. But everyone. Well, almost everyone. Not Mary Alice Watkins. Best to stay as far away from people like Mary Alice as possible. Look what happened to Ezra.

He suddenly felt more contented than he had in days. And after a few more minutes of this kind of reflection, he returned to William Baffin. The events of the morning behind him now.

In his first year as a whaler, *he read*, William Baffin served as pilot aboard the flagship of the whaling fleet—

Robert's breath left him as he finished the sentence.

—*The Tiger*.

EIGHT

If This Wasn't Swashbuckling,
He Didn't Know What Was!

It was only a coincidence. He knew that. Just one of those funny things that happened from time to time. Like last week. He'd been thinking about Claire's brother, Martin. Hadn't heard from the man in over six months. And then the mail arrived and there was Martin's letter. Right along with the phone bill and a flyer from Coolidge Farm and Feed.

There was no connection, of course. No connection between thinking about the man and his writing. No hocus-pocus or hoodoo. It was simply a coincidence. Just one of those funny things.

William Baffin worked on a ship called *The Tiger*. So what? It didn't mean a thing. Nothing.

And yet, Robert couldn't shake the feeling that if he swiveled the rocker so that he could look out the window, the tiger would be there. Looking straight at him. That the animal had moved to keep him in its sight. That it had used all its tiger sensors to locate him. To find him where he was right now. In his own living room. Minding his own business in the swivel rocker.

He could sense the tiger's eyes focused directly on him. Hear its feral panting. Feel its hot, animal breath on the back of his neck.

He sat without moving. Without blinking. A rabbit under the spell of a cobra. His breath coming in short, jagged spurts.

But this was crazy! He wasn't going to waste what little time he had left playing cat and mouse with an imaginary tiger! After all, he wasn't a child, was he? He wasn't Christopher Robin romping around in the Hundred Acre Wood.

But wasn't there a tiger in those woods, too?

Stop it, Robert! Get a hold of yourself!

He stood up, the rocker nodding and pitching behind him. He'd show whoever set up this little charade what he was made of. Now he marched—yes, marched!—back to the shelf that held the encyclopedias. Not even a quick sideways peek toward the window. Ha! Still in charge. Good! Good for him! If this wasn't swashbuckling, he didn't know what was!

He lifted the volume to its rightful place. Was it heavier than when he had taken it from the shelf? Never mind about that. He had done it! Walked across the room steady as a soldier. Eyes straight ahead. Not wavering an inch from his path. It had been difficult. It had been *very* difficult. Still, he hadn't looked for the tiger.

But the effort had not been without cost. He felt hot, feverish.

A splash of cool water. That's what he needed. He was just about to walk toward the half-bath when, without warning, he thought he was going to be sick. Right then. Right there. All over himself and the hooked rug they'd commissioned from that woman on the Maine coast.

The tumor.

He steadied himself against the shelving, breathing deeply, working hard to regain control. He'd always bragged that he had an iron stomach. Now he had no stomach at all. But he would hold on. He wasn't always able to, but this time, he would. He wasn't going to spoil that rug.

Eventually, the queasiness passed, snuck away on all fours, supple as an alley cat. It had taken every ounce of what was left of his willpower not to throw up.

Damned cancer!

But even as he cursed his illness, he knew it wasn't the tumor that had brought on the nausea. Not solely, anyway. It was the dream. A nightmare, really. He'd had it, he guessed, when he was napping earlier. But only remembered it when he'd tucked the encyclopedia back in its place.

It had come to him all at once, too. As if it had been there all along. Hidden. Waiting. Like a magician's grotesque assistant appearing from behind a shimmering veil.

When Robert was in the fifth grade, his teacher taught an alarming lesson on the developing world's expanding population. She was a large woman, her calves and ankles bound by thick support stockings she rolled to just beneath her knees.

"Think of it!" she'd commanded her pupils as she hauled herself up and down the aisles. "If all the citizens of China lined up single file and started walking into the ocean, the line would never end."

The fifth-grade Robert had missed the point entirely. *Why would the Chinese do such a horrible thing?* he'd wondered. *Who would make them?*

As an adult, he understood his teacher's lesson was more about her racism than a lesson in the demographics of Asia. Her fears of the Yellow Horde overtaking the Earth. Destroying the culture of the West. Obliterating everything America stood for.

But that understanding hadn't stopped the dreadful image from staying with him all his life. It popped up at odd moments. Often, just as he was about to fall asleep. Now it had found its way into a dream.

Uncountable numbers of Chinese walking toward an immense sea. One behind the other.

Men.

Women.

Toddlers.

Peasants.

Even emperors in their tall lacquered hats. Each waiting his or her turn to disappear beneath the dark water.

The figures moved silently. As if propelled by the forces of a powerful, unseen magnet. Robert was ashamed to admit it: his dream Chinese were . . . well, they were inscrutable. As unreadable to him, to the dreamer, as Braille. Too many of the Fu Man Chu novels he loved as a kid, he supposed.

But that wasn't all.

Each held a cushion. A small, silk pillow—was it red?—that rested waist-high on the flat of their outstretched palms. And on each cushion a single object.

Some of these Robert had not thought of in perhaps as many as sixty years. Yet they were as familiar, as intimate, as the touch of his hand.

A pocketknife his grandfather had given him when he was a boy.

A mug, chipped at the rim, that he had used when he was a college student.

A Beatles album.

Others were more recent. Some, in fact, he could easily locate in this very house.

A garden trowel.

The belt he bought last week.

A CD of the Bach cello suites.

Everything he had ever owned or touched or loved. Most sinking with its somber bearer into the black water. But some—books, album covers, a term paper he wrote in graduate school, even receipts for beloved articles of clothing—floating on its surface. Drifting on invisible currents toward a pale horizon.

Robert lifted his head. He looked at the books once more. He understood now. Understood what the dream was trying to tell him: He would never open those encyclopedias again. For years, their faded spines, their faint smell of must, their thin, brittle pages had been part of his life, and part of his life with Claire. *17 Across: Australia's longest river. 47 Down: The language of the Maya.* But this time when he walked away from the bookshelf, chances were he would never touch or think of them again.

NINE

As Speckled as a Trout

He had known, of course, that all of this would be lost. Known it for months. But he had known it only in a general way. DEATH with capital letters. That kind of thing. Now, suddenly, it was all lowercase.

And Claire.

He saw now that as his illness progressed, it was not only the wholeness of her that he would lose, Claire as Claire. But all the lovely particles of her, too. The wisp of hair that in fifty-some years had not stayed tucked behind her ear. The strawberry mole on her calf. The barely perceptible way she shifted her weight when her knee was hurting her.

And even the space she'd left behind. Devastating as it was, he loved it. Loved it in the way he might have loved an impaired child. Fiercely. Tenderly. But in the winding offices of his memory, it too would have an appointed last hour.

A pain, sharp as a bullet, shot through his stomach. That *was* the tumor. He had to sit down.

Below the shelf on which the encyclopedias rested, was another shelf, taller than the others. Photo albums. Twenty or more of them. Stacked. Leaning. Some, their cellophane pages loose and falling out. Others, more recent editions, tidy as a new Bible.

Robert had promised himself that he

would stay away from these albums. But he saw now it was a promise he could not keep. He grabbed the one closest to his hand, red like the pillows in the dream, and carried it to the maple desk.

He took a moment and breathed into the pain the way the therapist had taught him. Then, he opened the cover. The trip to Japan. Over twenty years ago.

Some of the snapshots had faded into mere ghosts of themselves. But many were still clear, even if the colors were so saturated they looked as if a child had taken crayons to them.

Claire. Feeding the deer at the park in Nara. (They'd practically stampeded her.)

Him. Hamming it up at the Tsukiji Fish Market.

Both of them. Holding hands in front of the Kiyomizu Temple. (He remembered exactly the older man they'd asked to take the picture. Claire had picked him out of the crowd. A Japanese professor of history who spoke perfect English.)

But what was that one? He leaned toward the album, bringing his face closer to the picture. Claire, standing in a shop of some kind. He remembered the skirt she was wearing. Plaid. Blue and yellow. He had always liked it, but she complained it made her hips look wide.

He tried to recall the day the photo had been taken, studying the long, skinny rectangle that was hanging just over her left shoulder in the snapshot. What was it? He opened the desk drawer and took out a large magnifying glass.

It was coming back to him now. The tour guide had planned a trip to a sumo village. But he and Claire had played hookey, wanting to spend some time away from the swarm of schoolmarms the tour had attracted.

They'd stumbled upon a small gallery. Japanese art. Scrolls. The kind that Japanese hung in their *tatami* rooms. The ones that were done with ink and those broad brushstrokes. And that must be what was hanging in the background, what had puzzled him just a few seconds earlier. A scroll.

He brought the glass close to his eye. Then moved it toward the picture, working to bring it into sharper focus. Just what he'd thought. It *was* a scroll.

If he steadied his hand, he might even be able to identify the image painted on it. Yes! A landscape of some kind. A full moon hanging over a set of cragged peaks. Lovely, really. Even twenty years later. Even in miniature.

But what was that in the foreground? He moved the glass down to bring the image more fully into the center of his vision. And there it was. Magnified. Looking directly at him. As if it had jumped into the photo that very moment. A tiger.

This time Robert didn't gasp. His heart didn't quicken. It was almost as if he'd been expecting it. As if a hidden self had guided his hand to choose that particular album from all the others. Had directed him to focus on that particular photograph.

He looked up from the photograph and rested his hand on the desk, his fingers still wrapped around the black handle of the magnifying glass. He let his gaze fall to the constellation of age spots that mottled the back of his hand.

When they were young, Claire had always marveled at the clarity of his skin, as flawless, nearly, as that porcelain sink. But over the last few years that had changed. He'd become as speckled as a trout.

He remembered now that the public television show had made a point of saying that it wasn't just the tiger's fur that was striped, but its very skin.

And then it hit him. An idea so alien that for a moment he really did wonder if he was losing his mind.

It's me, he thought. ***I am the tiger.***

TEN

Just a Little Time

When Miles arrived, Robert was ready. The library books piled in a neat pyramid on the kitchen counter, and on top of them, a pamphlet from the Historical Society.

"Anybody home?"

Robert loved the sound of the boy's voice. As an adolescent, it had been as high as a girl's. But after the dark mysteries of puberty, he had taken on the rich timbre of a *basso profundo*. A man's voice. And he loved to show it off. Loved to talk.

He could sing, too. It had been one of Robert and Claire's favorite domestic pleasures. Listening to Miles croon along with a tune on the radio as he cleaned out a flower bed or painted a fence.

"You should sing in an opera," Claire said to him.

"Maybe, Mrs. S," he'd answered. "If you mean the Grand Ole Opry."

Robert stepped into the kitchen to see him standing in the doorway, filling it up, as if the molding were a picture frame. Recently, Robert had begun to think of him as he had looked at fourteen. All arms and legs and torso. But it was a man now who stood in his kitchen. Twenty-three years old as of last week.

"Hey, Mr. S. Everything good? You feeling okay?"

Miles flicked his eyes over to the windowsill, the bottles.

"I'm fine, Miles. You don't have to worry about me."

"Who said I was worried? You're gonna be all right. Just need a little time to get feeling good again. That's all."

Robert looked down to pick at some imaginary lint on the cuff of his shirtsleeve. Did Miles actually believe that? Or was he protecting himself and Robert, too, from a truth he couldn't face?

Claire had been the closest thing to a mother Miles had, this relationship starting the day they'd hired Art to build the bookshelves. "Might have to bring the boy along," the man had said. "His mother is gone. Bad heart. Left me and the boy alone. But he won't give you no trouble."

From the moment they met Claire

and Miles were bound to one another. "Ain't never seen him take to no one like that," Art had said. "No one." Funny. It wasn't until that moment that Robert understood how much Claire had wanted a child of her own.

Losing Claire had been nearly as hard on the boy as it had been on Robert. Not that such things can be measured. Even when Claire could no longer recognize him, her skin translucent as rice paper, her mind opaque as coal, Miles wouldn't give in. He'd often said about Claire what he had just said to Robert about himself. *She just needs a little time to get feeling good again, Mr. S. To get back to herself. Just a little time. That's all.*

When Robert looked up, Miles had all three books in one hand. "I was planning on prunin' those apple trees today. We goin' to the library?"

"We are," Robert answered. "And to the Historical Society. And the bank."

Miles picked up the pamphlet. Read the title. "Annie Upton Cogswell: Photograph Collection of Old Houses and Their History."

"I thought I might do some research on the house," Robert explained. "Never got around to it. And you know how Mary Lynn Hanwell is about those pamphlets. She worries more about them than she does her own kids. I'd better get it back to the historical society before she calls the FBI."

"Maybe I could do it for you," Miles offered. "The research." With his free hand, he reached out and touched the wall to his left. It was just that kind of tender gesture that reminded Robert so much of Claire. "I love this old house," Miles said.

"I know you do," Miles answered.

He also knew something else. Something that Miles didn't know. The house was his, Miles's. Claire and he had decided that long ago. The house, the land, everything. That was why their last stop today would be the bank. Robert wanted to put an extra copy of the will in the safe deposit box.

"We'd better get moving," Robert said, stepping out of his slippers and into his canvas loafers. "Especially if you want to get to those trees. I also need to run into Lambert's."

Lambert's was what passed in the

village for a grocery. Iceberg lettuce and Wonder Bread mostly. Robert wanted some yogurt. Even though chances were, its expiration date would have gone by.

Miles gave a disapproving scrunch of his forehead.

With his free hand, he tapped out the errands on the counter. "Library. Historical Society. Bank. Lambert's. That's an awful lot in one day. You sure you're up to all that?"

"You know, Miles," Robert said, walking past him and out the door, "You're starting to sound a lot like Mary Alice Watkins."

"That's okay with me, Mr. S.," Miles replied, following closely behind him. "As long as I don't start looking like her, too."

ELEVEN

That Made Two of Them

Tigers, it seemed, were everywhere.

In the library. Four of them racing around the base of a tree. Linda Pillsbury, the half-time librarian told him the poster was from a retelling of *Little Black Sambo*.

At Lambert's. In the cereal aisle. "They're grrrrrrreat!"

At the Historical Society. How many times had Robert passed by that picture of Calvin Coolidge hanging in its oak frame in the foyer? Why today did he stop to read the caption under the picture? "Calvin Coolidge, the 29th

President of the United States, holding his beloved pet, Tiger."

At the bank. His favorite teller, Ginger, wearing a tiger print blouse, the black and orange stripes amazingly like the tiger's he had seen in his roses.

And even in Miles's truck. On the radio as they rode up the hill, errands completed. "Kansas City faced the Detroit Tigers today in a…"

None of this surprised Robert.

In fact, the appearance of the tigers seemed less an intrusion than a revelation. It affirmed the course of action he had decided upon. A course of action affirmed further by Miles himself.

After he had pruned the trees, the boy stood in the breezeway, careful not to track in the sawdust and bits of bark that covered the thighs of his jeans, the sweet smell of apple wood wafting through the screen door like some expensive cologne.

"One of those branches was a lot bigger than I bargained for," he said, wiping the sweat from his forehead with the handkerchief that he always carried in his back pocket. "For a while there, I had a tiger by the tail."

Robert hadn't meant to worry Miles by his response, but he knew from the boy's expression that he had.

"That makes two of us," he'd said.

TWELVE

What Seemed Perfect in Japan

The red truck climbed and then disappeared over the rise. Eventually, it would slow and turn left into the gravel parking lot at the elementary school.

Robert stood at the window. Waiting until the truck vanished from sight. He thought about calling Emma. Reminding her to remind Miles to get that brake light fixed before he got a ticket. But he heard Claire telling him to stop being such a fussbudget, and decided against it.

They made a good couple, Miles and Emma. Opposites in many ways. But alike in all the things that mattered.

What changes would they make in the house, he wondered. He hoped they would leave the sink. Keep the books.

It was sentimental, he knew, to wish for such things. Silly, even. Why should they keep the sink if they wanted something more modern? And the books? Who knows? Maybe that tattooed nurse had been right. Maybe they *were* shooting out poison arrows. Something certainly had.

The important thing, the *only* important thing, really, was that they be happy. And of that he had no doubt. Miles had a gift for it. Claire had given him this.

And Emma, though she was young, had a good head on her shoulders. He imagined them together. Here in the house. They were younger, much younger than he and Claire had been. But in many ways so much more of the world. It was all those electronic gizmos, he supposed. The Candles and so on.

But Robert didn't allow himself to linger on such thoughts for long. He had to get ready for Mary Alice.

He had a plan.

Luckily, the *yukata* was hanging right where he'd remembered it. In the guest bedroom. With all the old winter coats.

That picture had made him think of it. The one of Claire in the shop. They'd bought the *yukata* that same day the photo was taken. At first, he'd resisted. It wasn't cheap. But Claire had convinced him. *Think how comfortable you'll be,* she'd said. *And you're always saying you wish you had a light robe. You can put it on after your bath. Just like Japanese men do. It will be a reminder of the trip. It's perfect.*

He'd had to admit that she was right. It was comfortable. A fine, light-weight cotton, the robe would be just the thing on a weekend morning in the summer.

But what had seemed perfect in Japan seemed silly in Vermont. Whenever he put on the robe, he couldn't get over the feeling that he was wearing women's clothing. He knew it was wrong. Knew that Japanese men wore their *yukatas* when they wanted to relax, or, as Claire had suggested, after a bath. Still, he was terrified that a neighbor would drop by and see him. It was a small town. He had to be careful. Next thing he knew, people would be spreading the rumor that he had gone to Japan a man, but come back a geisha.

"I'm too old to start cross-dressing," he'd finally said to Claire one morning, as he fidgeted with one of the wide sleeves. From that morning on, the *yukata* hung in the winter closet. Undisturbed until now.

He half expected to find the dragons printed so artfully on the fabric to be transmogrified into tigers. But no, dragons they remained. Their long tails winding around the robe in graceful yellow whorls.

He slipped off his shoes and socks, his trousers and shirt, stepped out of his underwear and put the *yukata* on.

Tying the sash loosely around his waist, he couldn't help but notice how much weight he had lost in the last month.

THIRTEEN

Flashing the Dickens out of Mary Alice Watkins

"Bob? Bob? Are you here, Bob?"

Mary Alice's voice clattered through the house. As jarring as a glass shattering on the counter.

"Bob?"

Louder this time. My god! The woman's voice was a secret weapon. Why worry about terrorists? Just get Mary Alice shouting at them. *Ahmed? Mohammed? Mehdi?* They'd be stone deaf before they could holler Allah Akbar.

"'I'll be down in a second, Mary Alice. Have a seat at the table if you want."

"I'll just put the stew right here," she bellowed. "On the counter." He swore he heard the neighbor's dog howl.

Mary Alice didn't hear him come in the kitchen. He caught her with her nose in the refrigerator. Her skinny rump pointed straight at him. (Talk about poison arrows!) When she turned around, her chin dropped to her collarbone. She didn't even have the good sense to be embarrassed at her snooping.

"Bob!" she said. Or tried to say. Her voice had caught in her throat.

"Mary Alice."

For a moment, neither of them said a word. He smiled, looking as innocent as a Girl Scout peddling her Do-Si-Dos. Mary Alice gawked at him as if he were a transvestite.

"Are you all right, Bob?" she finally croaked. Her eyes, normally small and squinty, had grown to the size of quarters.

"I'm perfectly fine, Mary Alice. Why do you ask?"

"But what's that you're wearing?" she said. Backlit by the open refrigerator, the woman was cast into the kind of light low-budget directors often employed to illuminate their monsters.

"This is a *yukata*, Mary Alice. It's Japanese." He put his hands on his hips so that she could get the full effect of the robe. The fabric fell in a way that made the dragons look as if they were on the prowl. "Would you mind closing the refrigerator door?" he said.

She didn't move. Couldn't. Stared at

his bare feet. Moved her glance up his bruised shins and skinny calves. On up past the hem of the *yukata*. Didn't stop till she got to the top of his head. Only then was she able to reach behind her and push the refrigerator door closed.

"Thank you," he said. He could see that she was recovering now. Her eyes retracting to their normal unpleasant size.

"What did you call that thing you're wearing?" she asked. "That yokel... yukele..."

"*Yukata*," he said. "Three syllables. Yu-ka-ta. Try it. Yu-ka-ta."

"I'm not going to try it. And I don't care what you call it," she said. "It looks like a woman's bathrobe!" She was angry now. Angry because she'd been shocked out of her wits by a dying man dressed in an article of foreign clothing. A man who ought to know better. "You ought to be ashamed of yourself. Running around in that… that thing. It's not decent. And put on some slippers, Bob. Bare feet aren't sanitary. Not in your condition."

"My condition?" Robert asked. "I'm not *pregnant*, Mary Alice."

Her eyes darted toward the door.

"What's wrong with you, Bob?"

"I think we both know the answer to that question, Mary Alice." He couldn't remember the last time he had so much fun.

"I just don't know why a grown man wants to go running around in a woman's nightie. That's all."

"Oh, it might look like a woman's

nightie," Robert said. "But it's not. Japanese men wear them all the time. Look at the dragons. Oriental dragons are symbols of good luck. I'll bet you didn't know that, did you?"

Mary Alice looked at the door again. This time taking a sideways step toward it. Her hip bumping the counter.

"Well, I wouldn't be taking any suggestions from any Japanese," she huffed. "I don't care what you say."

"Oh, I know you don't, Mary Alice," Robert said. "You don't care what anybody says. Or thinks. Or feels. You never have."

Once more, the woman's jaw dropped.

"But let's forget about that for the moment," he continued, "Let bygones be bygones and go back to the *yukata*. It *is* men's clothing. I can prove it."

With that, he stepped backward and with one fluid movement, let fall the *yukata*'s narrow sash, grabbed the sides of the robe and yanked them wide open, his arms stretched to either side. It was as if he had trained for it. Trained his whole life to flash the dickens out of Mary Alice Watkins.

The tumor sent a pain through his side, dirty as a rusty nail, but he held his ground. He thought about wiggling his hips a bit, but decided against it. No point in being dirty about it. That wasn't the point. No, standing there was enough. Standing there like a skinny Japanese angel.

For a moment, Robert thought he

had gone too far. Thought she was having a stroke. But eventually, the woman regained her breath, and, squawking like a goose, ran out of the house, arms akimbo.

Robert closed the robe and ran after her.

"By the way, Mary Alice," he called out as she scrambled into her Buick, "My name is Robert!"

FOURTEEN

It's All Tiger

If he doubted it was worth it, all he had to do was think about the look on Mary Alice Watkins's face. Like she'd been goosed. Not only that, but she actually squealed the Buick's tires as she pulled out of his driveway. He laughed so hard that for a few seconds he beat down the pain.

Claire would have disapproved of what he had done to Mary Alice. He knew that. But he also knew she wouldn't have been able to help herself: She would have laughed too. Might be laughing right now for all he knew.

He looked at the pot of lentil stew. Mary Alice nearly knocked it off in her haste to get out of the house. Next to it sat a pile of those homemade biscuits. Everyone in town knew about those biscuits. They showed up at every church supper, as unyielding to the tooth as the granite boulders that dotted the New England countryside. Mary Alice never seemed to notice that she took home as many biscuits as she brought. Or more likely, she didn't care.

Robert opened the cabinet doors under the sink, and dumped them, basket and all, into the trash. He was about to do the same with the lentil stew. But as he started to tilt the pot into the sink, he stopped. Lambert's hadn't had the yogurt. Why not the stew? It would do just as well. He moved the pot to the stove and lit the burner beneath it.

He went to the drawer beneath the dish cupboard, took out a clean place-mat and centered it in front of his chair at the kitchen table. Like the rocker in the living room, the table had been left behind by its former owners.

Of course! He was surprised he hadn't realized it earlier. The table's legs were turned of some kind of soft wood, but its surface was striped with bands of amber and a dark chestnut brown—tiger maple.

He needed a napkin, a spoon, a glass of water.

As he set the table, he remembered the short conversation he'd had with Miles just before the boy left.

He'd been watching from the breeze-way as Miles stood next to his truck, digging in his pocket for his keys.

"Miles?" he said through the screen.

"Mr. S.?"

"Maybe it's about time you started calling me by my first name. You know what it is, don't you?"

Miles paused. Then gave him that crooked are-you-crazy smile. Robert hadn't seen that smile for months. Since he got sick.

"Course I do," Miles said.

"Of course you do," Robert repeated. "It was a silly question."

Miles climbed into the cab of his truck. But before he started the engine, he unrolled the window on the passenger's side.

"See you tomorrow, then," he called out, "Robert."

More a balm to him than anything modern medicine had offered.

The stew was steaming now, filling the kitchen with the sharp aroma of curry. *Only Mary Alice*, he said aloud. By which he meant that only Mary Alice Watkins would serve curry to a man whose intestines had more stitches than an Amish quilt.

He walked back into the living room. There he took from the bookshelves one of the photo albums. But this time he chose carefully. He knew the one he wanted. It was the one he had put together himself. Claire. Baby pictures. Snapshots from her childhood. Her teen years. Her young adulthood. All their years together.

This he carried back to the kitchen and put next to the placemat. Now, he went to the cupboard and took a favorite bowl. An antique that had belonged to his grandmother. He filled this with the curried lentils. Finally, he turned to the windowsill and with both hands scooped up the bottles there.

He noticed with some pride that his hands weren't shaking as he emptied their contents into the lentils. He carried the bowl to the table, set it on the placemat, opened the photo album of Claire and sat down.

He had planned to go through the album one more time, but as he took the first bite, he found he didn't need to. He felt Claire here with him now. As close as she had ever been.

He kept his eyes turned to the window, wondering if he would see the tiger again. *His* tiger. The one that had come for him. But he knew it wasn't important. He didn't need to see it to know it was there.

He thought about the number of times he and Claire had heard something in the night. Some nameless thing that thumped or groaned or whined, then turned out to be nothing. Nothing. And yet they had heard it, hadn't they?

And hadn't everyone at one time or another *felt* something? Something hiding in the shadows? Something waiting. They couldn't see it, but that didn't mean it wasn't real.

He ate quickly. The stew was a much better choice than the yogurt. It was impossible to distinguish the bitter, undercooked lentils from the brightly colored pills and capsules. Mary Alice had been of real help at last.

He stood up now, carried the empty bowl to the sink, rinsed it and left it to dry on the drainboard. No sense in making a mess. He stopped, taking in the still life he'd created, the blue and white bowl, upside down on the porcelain drainboard.

Then, for the last time, Robert Louis Stevenson walked out the door of his house.

The grass was soft under his feet.

As he walked, he let the *yukata* fall to the ground, his nakedness becoming as natural a part of the landscape as the hemlocks and the maples. The sun had slipped behind a band of late afternoon clouds; its rays beamed down in stripes of light.

Tiger, he heard himself say.

Light was streaming, too, through the newly pruned apple trees.

It's all tiger.

He lay beneath the arbor, the stew taking its effect.

The cancer.

Mary Alice.

The sky.

The earth.

Tiger.

All of it tiger.

Ruthless.

Magnificent.

Unknowable.

Miles was tiger.

Strong.

Invincible.

And Claire.

More natural in her environment than anyone he had ever known.

Claire was tiger, too.

He closed his eyes.

He could see her face before him.

Now, he heard the soft, rhythmic thud of heavy paws padding toward him across the grass, and he was filled with an overwhelming sense of gratitude.

How lucky I have been.

This was what he was thinking when he felt the animal's teeth sink gently, gently into his mortal flesh. And what he was thinking, too, when it lifted and carried him, the way it might have a cub, to its distant, unapproachable lair.